THE ILLUSTRATIONS IN THIS BOOK WERE MADE DIGITALLY.

Cataloging—in—Publication Data has been applied for and may be obtained from the Library of Congress.

ISBN 978—1—4197—3634—6

Abrams Books for Young Readers are available at special discounts when purchased in quantity for premiums and promotions as well as fundraising or educational use. Special editions can also be created to specification. For details, contact specialsales@abramsbooks.com or the address below.

Abrams® is a registered trademark of Harry N. Abrams, Inc.

ABRAMS The Art of Books
195 Broadway, New York, NY 10007
abramsbooks.com

For Frenchtown—thank you. ♥
—J.McG.

For fellow marshmallow lovers.
—C.S.

It was Christmas Eve in Quirkville and everyone was eager and excited for Santa's visit. Reginald stuffed stockings for his zombie friends. Zarfon loaded his spaceship for a Christmas Day peanut butter delivery to his home planet. And Abigail Zink, the smartest girl in Quirkville, was on her computer, ready to follow Santa's progress.

All was well in Quirkville, until Abigail Zink read . . .

CHRISTMAS IS CANCELED!

The mayor called an emergency town meeting.
"Santa is stuck in a terrible storm," he said.

"We've got to help Santa out of that storm," said Reginald.
"SPLOINK!" said Zarfon.
"You're right, Zarfon," said Abigail Zink. "There's no time to lose. We can go with you to deliver your peanut butter and stop at the North Pole on the way."

"You sure have a lot of peanut butter in here," said Reginald.
"SPLOINK!" said Zarfon.
"Peanut butter *is* out of this world," said Abigail Zink.

But when they saw the North Pole . . .

. . . it was worse than they thought.

"I can hardly see Santa's workshop!" said Reginald.
"No wonder Santa couldn't ride his sleigh tonight,"
said Abigail Zink.

Zarfon tried to clear the windshield, but the wipers stuck. He tried to fly through the storm, but the engine clogged. The ship dipped and wobbled and spun through the storm until it landed atop Santa's gingerbread house.

"Thank peppermint you've come!" said Santa. "We're stuck!"

Reginald tried to wipe the snow from his eyes. "This snow is so *gooey*."

Abigail Zink let some fall on her tongue. "This snow is so *sugary*."

Zarfon poked a mound of squishy snow.

"SPLOINK?"

"This isn't snow," they said. "It's . . ."

"MARSHMALLOW!"

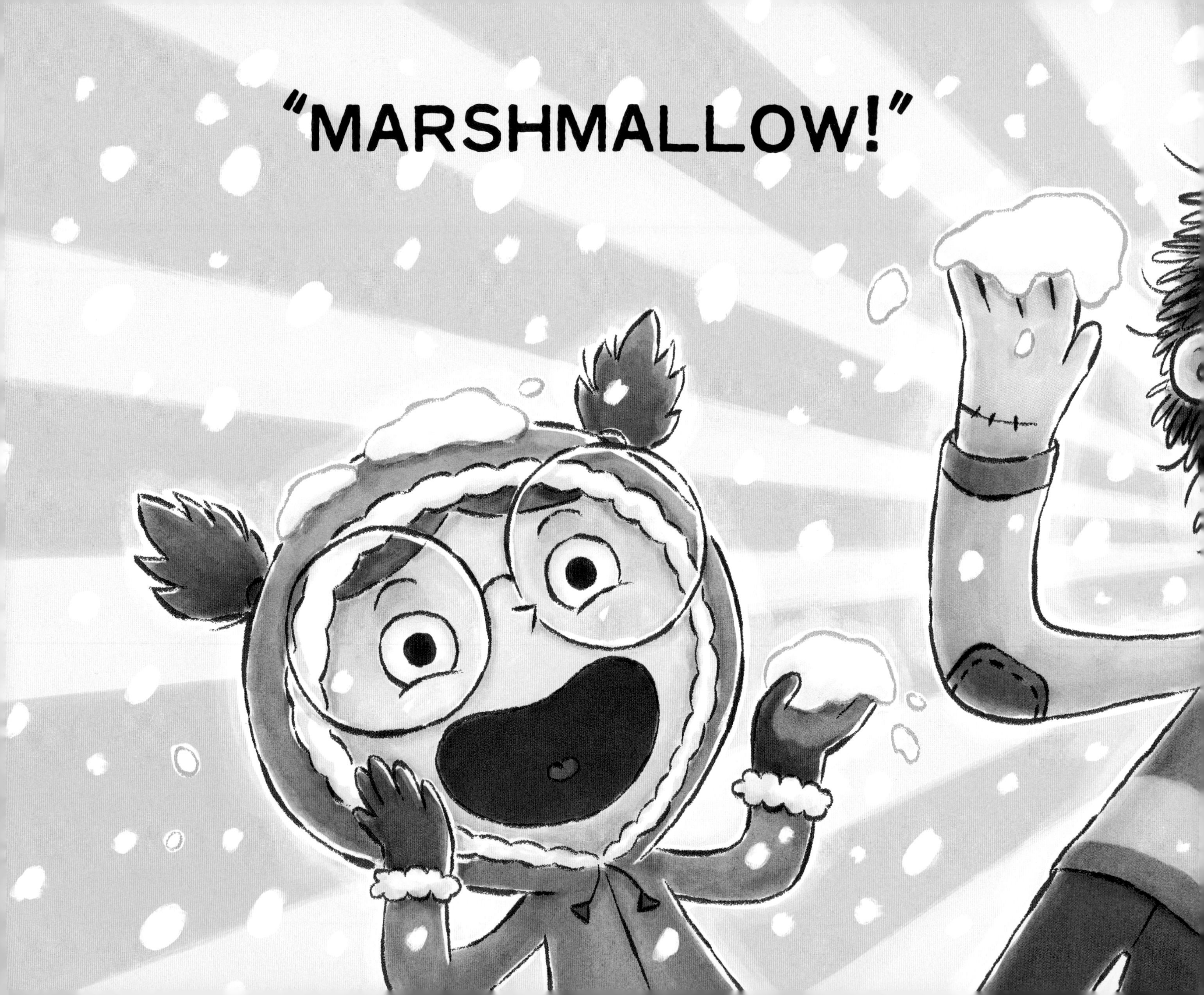

"Of course it is," said Santa Claus. "The marshmallow cream factory has gone bonkers!"

"JINGLE JINGLE!" exclaimed Santa's elves.

"We've got to stuff those chimneys," said Abigail Zink.

"JINGLE JINGLE?" asked the elves.

"SPLOINK!" said Zarfon.

"Good idea, Zarfon," said Reginald.
"We'll use the peanut butter from the ship!"

They gathered as many jars of peanut butter as they
could carry and rushed to the factory.
"Pack the chimneys with peanut butter," said Reginald.
"That'll stop it!"

No sooner had they finished than the building began to shake.
It began to shimmy. The factory gears groaned and the chimneys
choked. The whole building swelled and bellowed.
"JINGLE JINGLE!" hollered the elves.
"Hold on to your stockings!" said Santa. "It's going to . . ."

"Ho-ho-HO!" said Santa Claus, sticking a fingerful of peanut butter and marshmallow into his mouth. "This is SPLENDIFEROUS!"

"Yum!" said Reginald.

"Wowza!" said Abigail Zink.

"SPLOINK!" said Zarfon.

"JINGLE JINGLE!" said the elves.

"Now, we have to help clean up the North Pole so that Santa can deliver the presents," said Reginald. "But where will all this marshmallow go?"

"I know!" said Abigail Zink. "We'll make peanut butter and marshmallow sandwiches for everyone!"

It didn't take long for them to turn the marshmallow drifts into lots and lots and lots of sandwiches.

"There's still time to save Christmas!" said Abigail Zink.
"But my sleigh can't possibly carry both the presents and the sandwiches," said Santa.

"SPLOINK . . ." said Zarfon, pointing to his ship.
"But the engines are still clogged," said Reginald.

"I've got another idea," said Abigail Zink.
"JINGLE JINGLE!" said the elves.

"Merry Christmas to all and to all a good . . ."

"... sandwich!"

MERRY CHRISTMAS
FROM QUIRKVILLE!

From
Santa &
friends,
with
Love &
Yumminess